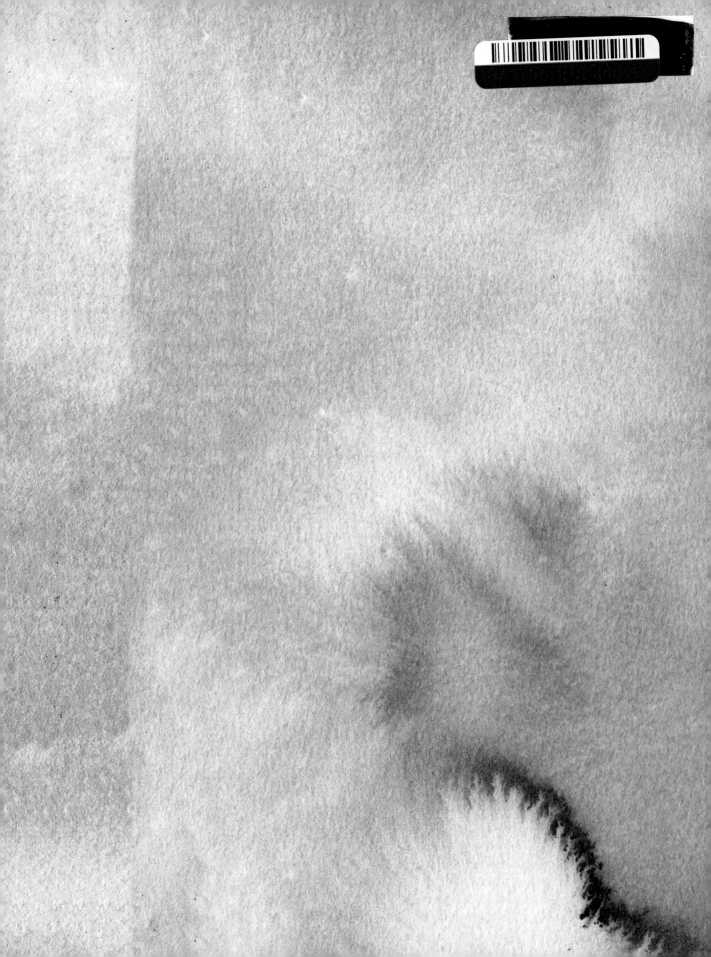

THIS BOOK IS DEDICATED TO MY FAMILY, FRIENDS, AND STUDENTS WHO HAVE PUSHED ME TO CONTINUE THIS JOURNEY WITH AMOYA.

www.mascotbooks.com

Amoya's Accent

For more information, please contact:
Mascot Books
620 Herndon Parkway, Suite 320
Herndon, VA 20170
info@mascotbooks.com

Library of Congress Control Number: 2020921556

CPSIA Code: PRT0321A
ISBN-13: 978-1-64543-779-6

Printed in the United States

AMOYA'S ACCENT

Written by
DAHLIA RICHARDS

Illustrated by
TERRI KELLEHER

"Two days I've been here at dis school, and all I can tink about is dis weather. I know Grandma Leah tell us seh outside get really cold, but I neva expect dis," I whisper to myself, staring out the foggy window. "Dis place is not at all like Jamaica! I tink my lips are still frozen together!"

"Amoya," calls Ms. Hamilton, interrupting my thoughts.

"Yes, Teacha?" I answer distractedly.

"What did the main character do that made her sister upset?"

"Teacha, she lick di icenin offa di spoon."

"Yes, Amoya, you are correct. She licked the icing off the spoon. And please, call me Ms. Hamilton."

"Yes, Ms. Hamilton."

I can hear Nicole and Shannon giggling across the room. I look over at them and wonder why they are laughing.

"Llevo dos días en la escuela y no hago más que pensar en el clima. Sé que mi abuela Leah nos dice que afuera hace mucho frio, pero nunca esperaba esto," susurra Amoya. "¡Este lugar no se parece en nada a Jamaica! ¡Creo que mi labios todavía están congelados!"

"Amoya," me llama la Sra. Hamilton interrumpiendo mis pensamientos.

"¿Si Maestra?" respondo distraída.

"¿Que hizo el personaje principal para enojar a su hermana?"

"Maestra, ella lamió la crema de la cuchara."

"Si, Amoya, tienes razón. Lamió la crema de la cuchara. Y por favor, llámame Sra. Hamilton."

"Si Sra. Hamilton."

Puedo oír a Nicole y Shannon riéndose desde el otro lado del salón. Las miro, preguntándome por qué se están riendo.

As soon as the bell rings, Ms. Hamilton lets us out of class. I put on my new sweater, my snow pants, my big, puffy jacket, my hat, and my gloves and wrap my scarf as close to my eyes as possible. I step outside and wait on the steps for my big sister, Denise, and my brother, Ryan, to come pick me up.

Nicole and Shannon walk by. They giggle as soon as they see me.

"Whachisofunny?" I ask them.

They giggle louder and keep walking.

Tan pronto como suena la campana, la Sra. Hamilton nos deja salir de clase. Me puse mi suéter nuevo, mis pantalones para la nieve, mi gran chaqueta mullida, mi gorra, mis guantes, y me puse la bufanda lo más cerca posible de mis ojos. Salgo y espero en los escalones a que mi hermana mayor, Denise, y mi hermano, Ryan, vengan a recogerme.

Nicole y Shannon pasan caminando. En cuanto me ven, se empiezan a reír.

"¿Queestangracioso?" les pregunto.

Sonríen más fuerte y siguen caminando.

"Come cross di street, Moya. Yuh know yuh don't need to tie di scarf all di way to your eyes, right?" says Denise. "And why yuh looking at dose girls like dat?" she continues.

I pull my scarf down and reply, "Because dey always lookin' at me and laughin'. I don't know what's wrong wid dem!"

"Laughin' for what? Don't mek likkle tings like dat badda yuh," she comforts me.

She gives my hand a little squeeze, and we start to walk home.

"Ven a cruzar la calle, Moya. Sabes que no necesitas cubrirte los ojos con la bufanda, ¿verdad?" dice Denise.

"¿Y por qué miras a las chicas así?" ella continua.

Me bajo la bufando y respondo, "Porque siempre me miran y se ríen. ¡No se qué les pasa!"

"¿Riéndose de qué? No dejes que las cosas pequeñas te molesten," ella me consuela.

Ella me agarra fuerte la mano y empezamos a caminar a casa.

The next day, Ms. Hamilton gives us a times table review. If there's anything I know, it's my times tables! In Jamaica, we start learning them in grade 2, kind of like a song: "2 ones 2, 2 twos 4, 2 threes 6."

"What is five times four?" Ms. Hamilton quizzes us.

"Twenty!" we all shout.

"What's three times one?"

"Tree!" I yell a little too loudly.

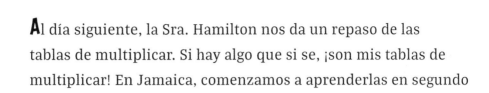

Al día siguiente, la Sra. Hamilton nos da un repaso de las tablas de multiplicar. Si hay algo que si se, ¡son mis tablas de multiplicar! En Jamaica, comenzamos a aprenderlas en segundo grado como una canción, "2 por uno 2, 2 por dos, 4, 2 por tres, 6.

"¿Cuanto son cinco por cuatro?" Sra. Hamilton nos pregunta.

"¡Veinte!" gritamos todos.

"¿Cuanto son tres por uno?"

"¡Tre!" grito yo, un poco fuerte.

"Did you hear the way she said three?" whispers Shannon.

"Yea, she said it like the trees outside!" Nicole giggles.

Ms. Hamilton sternly looks at both of them. "Ladies," she warns them, "be kind!"

I don't think there's anything wrong with the way I say three. "Tree, tree," I repeat under my breath. I sit quietly for the rest of the review.

"¿Escuchaste la forma en que dijo tres?" susurra Shannon.

"¡Si, ella lo dijo como los arboles afuera!" Nicole se ríe.

La Sra. Hamilton las mira severamente a ambas. "Senoritas," las advierte, "sean amables."

No creo que haya nada malo con la forma en como digo tres. "Tre, tre," repito en voz baja. Me quedo en silencio durante el resto del la clase.

Later during language arts, I hear Nicole snicker as I read the word vegetable.

"Veggie-te-ble. Veggie-teble." Am I saying it wrong? Is this really why Nicole and Shannon keep laughing at me? What is wrong with those two?

I put away my books when Nicole and Shannon walk by my desk. "Why yuh always laughin' afta me? Yuh makin' fun of di way I talk?" I ask them. They look at each other and start to giggle again. I quickly close my desk and head to my locker.

Ms. Hamilton gives me a knowing look as I walk out the door. "Nicole and Shannon, stop by my desk, please."

Más tarde, durante lengua y literatura, escucho a Nicole reírse mientras leo la palabra vegetales.

"Ve-hi-ta-les. Vehi-ta-les." ¿Lo estoy diciendo mal? ¿Es por eso que Nicole y Shannon se siguen riendo de mi? ¿Qué les pasa a esas dos?"

Guardo mis libros cuando Nicole y Shannon pasan a lado de mi pupitre. "¿Por qué siempre se ríen de mi? ¿Se burlan de mi forma de hablar?" les pregunto. Se miran y comienzan a reírse de nuevo. Rápidamente, cierro mi pupitre y me dirijo a mi casillero.

La Sra. Hamilton me mira con complicidad mientras salgo por la puerta. "Nicole y Shannon, vengan a mi escritorio por favor."

As I walk to catch up with Denise and Ryan, I look back and see Nicole and Shannon come out of the building with a not-so-happy look on their faces. I hope Ms. Hamilton let them have it!

"Those two still givin' yuh trouble?" Denise asks me.

"Dey keep laughin' every time I talk. Di teacha call to dem when we were leavin'."

"Why de tink people haffi soun' like dem?" Ryan questions. He takes a good look at them before we head home.

Mientras camino para alcanzar a Denise y Ryan, miro hacia atrás y veo que Nicole y Shannon salen del edificio con una expresión no muy feliz en sus caras. !Espero que la Sra. Hamilton les cantara las cuarenta!

"¿Te siguen dando problemas?" me pregunta Denise.

"Siguen riéndose cada vez que hablo. La maestra las llamó cuando nos íbamos."

"¿Por qué creen que toda la gente necesita hablar como ellas?" pregunta Ryan.

Ryan les echa una buen mirada antes de regresar a casa.

We walk into class the next morning, and Ms. Hamilton seems really excited.

"I have a special lesson for us today," she beams. She hits play, and we see some people singing:

"One and two and three and four, up and down and around we go!"

Each time there's a new singer, they sound different from the person before! One lady even sounds like my Grandma Leah!

"What do we notice about the video so far?" asks Ms. Hamilton as she hits pause.

Nicole yells out, "They all talk funny!" and starts to giggle. Shannon, of course, has to join her. Ms Hamilton gives them the look.

"They do not talk funny," corrects Ms. Hamilton. "This video is about accents."

A la mañana siguiente, entramos en clase y la Sra. Hamilton parece muy emocionada.

"Tengo una lección especial hoy", dice ella. Ella pone un video y vemos a gente cantando:

"Uno y dos y tres y cuatro, arriba, y abajo, ¡y alrededor y vamos!" La misma canción suena una y otra vez.

¡Cada vez hay un nuevo cantante que suena muy diferente de la persona anterior! ¡Hasta uno sonó como mi abuela Leah!

"¿Qué han notado sobre el video hasta ahora?" pregunta la Sra. Hamilton.

Nicole grita, "¡Todos hablan gracioso!" y comienza a reírse. Shannon, por supuesto hace lo mismo La Sra. Hamilton las mira.

"No hablan gracioso," corrige La Sra. Hamilton. "El video trata de los acentos."

I raise my hand.

"Yes, Amoya?" calls Ms. Hamilton.

"All di singers had different accents. Some of dem said 'fur' or 'foor.' Well, dat's what it soun' like to me. I tink dey all come from different places."

"You are absolutely right, Amoya! We all have an accent, and what it sounds like depends on where you live or have lived," Ms. Hamilton explains.

"Now, turn to your table groups. I want you all to think of your own families. Does everyone in your family sound the same? Has anyone moved here from somewhere else?"

Levanto la mano.

"¿Si, Amoya?" dice la Sra. Hamilton.

Todos los cantantes tenían diferentes acentos. Algunos de ellos decían "cuátro" o "cuatró", bueno, eso es lo que me pareció. Creo que todos vienen de diferentes lugares.

"¡Tienes toda la razón, Amoya! Todos tenemos acento depende de donde vivas o hayamos vivido", explica la Sra. Hamilton.

"Ahora, diríjanse a sus grupos de mesa. Quiero que todos piensen en sus familias. ¿Todos en sus familias hablan igual? ¿Alguien se ha mudado aquí desde otro lugar?"

Of course, Nicole has to end up in my group. I start by reminding them that my family just moved here from Jamaica. Bo-Ra talks about how sometimes people ask her mother to repeat things even though she's been in America for fifteen years. Natalie was born in Puerto Rico, and her parents speak mostly Spanish. They still have their accents, too, even though she doesn't sound the same as them.

We finish talking at our tables.

"I heard some great conversations in your groups," comments Ms. Hamilton. "Let's move into our sharing circle."

We all come to the rug and sit in a circle facing each other.

Por supuesto, Nicole tiene que estar en mi grupo. Comienzo recordándoles que mi familia acaban de llegar de Jamaica. Bo-Ra habla de cómo a veces la gente le pide a su mamá que repita las cosas, a pesar de llevar quince años viviendo en los Estados Unidos. Natalie nació en Puerto Rico y sus padres hablan principalmente español. Todavía tienen sus acentos también, aunque ella no suena igual que ellos.

Terminamos de hablar con nuestros grupos. "Escuche una gran conversación en sus grupos," comenta la Sra. Hamilton. "Pasemos a nuestro Circulo de Compartir".

Todos llegamos a la alfombra y nos sentamos en un circulo.

"**A** successful circle follows these guidelines. We speak and listen from the heart. We talk only when we have the talking piece. We speak from an 'I' perspective, sharing our own truths," she reminds us.

"I noticed that we are not being the kind, welcoming, third-grade community that we agreed we should be at the beginning of the year," she starts. "Let's share our thoughts on this. How does it feel when someone is unkind to you?"

She passes the talking piece to Marco. The talking piece is a small quilt made from pieces of old t-shirts from each student.

"**P**ara tener un circulo exitoso, seguimos estas normas. Hablamos y escuchamos desde el corazón. Hablamos solo cuando tenemos el objeto para hablar. Hablamos desde un perspectiva nuestra, compartiendo nuestras verdades," nos recuerda.

"Me he dado cuenta de que no somos la comunidad bienvenida de tercer grado que acordamos ser al principio del año," comienza. "Compartamos nuestros pensamientos sobre esto. ¿Cómo te sientes cuando alguien es cruel contigo?"

Ella le pasa el objeto a Marco. El objeto es una pequeña colcha con trozos de las camisetas viejas de cada estudiante.

"I don't like when people make fun of other people. Everyone is different, and that's okay," Marco says.

When the quilt gets to me, I sit up straight. "I don't like it when some people laugh when I talk. I soun' different because, like we saw in the video, yuh soun' like di people you live aroun', and I don't think there's anything wrong with dat. All of you soun' different to me, and dat's okay. People shouldn't make fun of other people."

I can feel my eyes getting watery, so I pass the quilt to Alex.

"No me gusta cuando las personas se burlan de otras personas. Todos somos diferentes y eso está bien."

Cuando me llega la colcha, me senté derecha en el piso. "No me gusta cuando algunas personas se ríen cuando hablo. Sueno diferente porque, como vimos en el video, suenas como la gente con la que vives, y no hay nada malo en eso. Para mí, todos ustedes suenan diferentes y está bien. La gente no debería burlarse de otras personas".

Puedo sentir mis ojos llenándose de lagrima, así que paso la colcha a Alex.

Nicole and Shannon are looking at me when I look up. I can tell from their faces that they feel bad. I look over at Ms. Hamilton, and she gives me a nod. We wrap up our circle as the bell rings.

Nicole y Shannon me miran cuando levanto la vista. Puedo ver por sus expresiones que se sienten mal. Miro a la Sra. Hamilton y ella me asiente. En cuanto terminamos nuestro circulo, suena la campana.

As I make my way outside to meet Denise and Ryan, Nicole and Shannon walk over and stop right in front of me.

"Amoya, I'm sorry I made fun of the way you talk," Nicole apologizes.

"Me, too, Amoya. We didn't realize that everyone has an accent—even people that come from different parts of America. We didn't mean to hurt your feelings," adds Shannon.

"Tanks. I'm glad we all learn someting today." I smile and cross the street to meet Ryan and Denise.

Al salir para encontrarme con Denise y Ryan, Nicole y Shannon se acercan y se detienen enfrente mia.

"Amoya, lamento haberme burlado de tu forma de hablar," se disculpa Nicole.

"Yo también, Amoya. No sabíamos que todos tenemos acentos, incluso las personas que vienen de diferentes partes de Estados Unidos. No teníamos la intención de herir tus sentimientos," agrego Shannon.

"Gracias. Me alegra que todos aprendimos algo hoy." Sonreí y crucé la calle para encontrarme con Ryan y Denise.

"What was dat about?" asks Ryan.

I tell them that Ms. Hamilton shared a video about accents and how we all got to talk about it afterward.

"Nicole and Shannon even said sorry jus' now."

"Well, I'm glad yuh fix it cause I can't have people pickin' on my likkle sista," he says with a big grin.

Denise and I kiss our teeth at him and start walking home.

Old, big-head Ryan! I can't wait to write to our cousin Nadine! She will definitely want to hear about my first days in Chicago!

"¿Que pasaba?" pregunta Ryan.

Les dije que la Sra. Hamilton compartió un video con nosotros de los acentos y como después todos pudimos hablar sobre ello.

"Nicole y Shannon me acaban de pedir perdón."

"Bueno. Me alegro de que este solucionado, porque no puedo permitir que la gente atormente a mi hermana," dice Ryan con una gran sonrisa. Denise y yo nos chupamos los dientes y comenzamos a caminar a casa.

¡Que soberbio es Ryan! ¡Estoy impaciente por escribir a nuestra prima Nadine! ¡Estoy segura que querrá saber come han sido mis primeros días en Chicago!

RECIPE FOR A WARM DRINK ON COLD DAYS:

While Horlicks was my favorite drink as a child, Milo has become my favorite bedtime beverage as an adult.

Ingredients
- 1 1/2 cups of milk (your choice)
- 2 tablespoons of Milo
- 1 teaspoon of brown sugar (to taste)

Directions
Bring milk to a boil on the stove top or in the microwave. Remove thin film from milk. Mix in Milo and sugar. Enjoy!

About the Author

Dahlia Richards is the author of *Amoya's Big Move*, and now the sequel, *Amoya's Accent*. She writes to connect the many students from different countries present in her fifth-grade language arts classes. Dahlia believes moving is a universal experience and shares her stories in both English and Spanish. She currently lives in Evanston with her husband Alex. Find her at **meetamoya.com**.

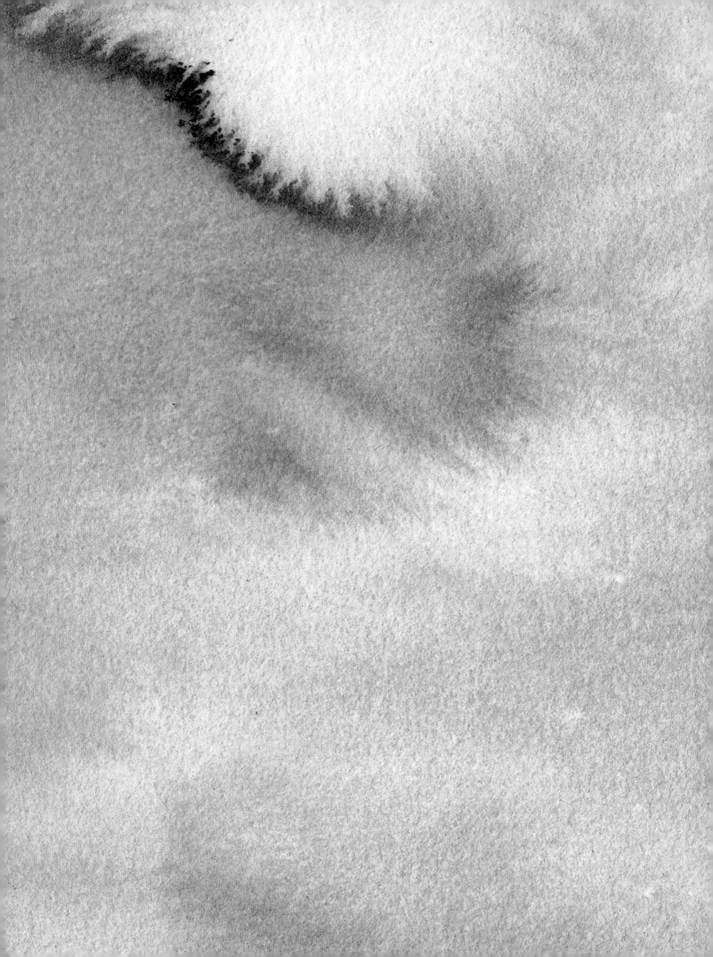